Dedicated to the fancy cat I met in the Paris Metro

and my two moms,

Elsie Raymond and Helen Arnold

—M. D. A.

For Cathy, Ray, and Michael Ann

—J. E. D.

Library of Congress Cataloging-in-Publication Data
Arnold, Marsha Diane.
Metro cat / by Marsha Diane Arnold ; illustrated by Jack E. Davis.
p. cm.
Summary: When Sophie, the cover cat for Fancy Cat Magazine,
is stranded in a Paris Metro station, she must learn to fend for herself.
ISBN 0-307-10213-0 (alk. paper)
[1. Cats—Fiction. 2. Subways—France—Paris—Fiction. 3. Self-reliance—Fiction.
4. Paris (France)—Fiction.] I. Davis, Jack E., ill. II. Title.
PZ7.A7363 Me 2001   [E]—dc21   00-056173

The illustrations for this book
were created with watercolor, acrylic, and colored pencil.

Metro Cat

To Benjamin—
Fancy that!
Fancy Cat!
Marsha
Diane
Arnold

Meow
↑
Victoria

by MARSHA DIANE ARNOLD
illustrated by JACK E. DAVIS

A Golden Book ✧ New York

Golden Books Publishing Company, Inc., New York, New York 10106

Sophie LeBeque was the fanciest cat in Paris. Posters of her draped in diamond collars hung in Paris bus stops and store windows . . . even on the walls of the Metro, the Parisian subway.

Sophie led a hectic life as the Cover Cat for *Fancy Cat* magazine. She liked the attention. But the thing Sophie loved most about her life was her sunroom, where she ate fresh trout for breakfast, played in a catnip garden, and napped overlooking the River Seine.

One morning, Sophie's butler announced, "You have a 7 A.M. photo session, Mademoiselle LeBeque! We must hurry to catch the morning light at the Eiffel Tower. I'll drape you in diamonds when we get there."

"I haven't had my fresh trout breakfast," meowed Sophie.

But the butler did not hear. He placed Sophie in her

silk-lined carrying case, hurried to the limousine, and sped into the streets of Paris. Sophie's cage slid from side to side. "Please don't rush," she meowed.

But the limousine screeched around a corner, the back door flew open, and Sophie's cage sailed out.

It bounced onto the street, teetered at the top of a staircase, tumbled down . . .

BONG . . . BONG . . . BONG, jarred

open, and toppled Sophie into a swirling sea of shoes.

Sophie LeBeque, the fanciest cat in Paris, was in the middle of the Metro's morning rush hour.

Pointy blue heels scrunched her toes.

Scruffy tennis shoes smashed her tail.

"MEOWCH!!!" shrieked Sophie.

A wave of brown loafers pushed Sophie further down a long hallway. A swinging briefcase sent her spinning into a corner.

Catching her breath, Sophie peered through the crowd. On the opposite wall was a poster of the June issue of *Fancy Cat* magazine, with Sophie posed next to the *Mona Lisa* at the Louvre.

Sophie meowed to the crowd, "I'm Sophie LeBeque, the fanciest cat in Paris. Please stop rushing and help me find my butler."

Click-click, squish-squish, shuffle-shuffle. The shoes rushed past.

Just then, Sophie's nose caught a tantalizing smell mingled with the scent of rubber soles and leather shoes. Running to catch their trains, the crowds munched breakfast. Here and there, a bit of baguette, a chunk of croissant, a piece of apple tart dropped between their shoes.

I didn't have my fresh trout this morning, Sophie remembered.

Cautiously, Sophie moved into the crowd.

She skipped by a sandal, leaped over a boot, and sidestepped an oxford to reach a taste of cream puff.

She scampered across a sneaker for a bite of chocolate crepe, darted around a platform shoe for a nibble of eclair, then scurried back to her corner and fell asleep, exhausted, on the floor.

The next day, Sophie tried to decide what to do. But her butler and *Fancy Cat* magazine had always told her what to do before. So in the Metro Sophie stayed.

She didn't like sleeping on the cold floor, and it was hectic rushing through shoes for breakfast. But Sophie made a game of when to rush in and when not to.

Soon she became so light on her feet that her paws were never scrunched and her tail never smashed. Twirling around a tennis shoe, swirling past a pump, and waltzing over a wingtip for a morsel of quiche became almost as much fun as playing in her catnip garden.

One morning after breakfast, Sophie noticed a man plastering a new poster on the wall, right over hers!

The morning light shone through the Eiffel Tower, making Monique's fur sparkle like her diamond collars.

Sophie LeBeque stared at the poster a long time.

But soon a familiar *click-click, squish-squish, shuffle-shuffle* sound entered her ears. She noticed a bit of baguette falling to the floor and rushed in after it.

Sophie scurried through one pair of shoes after another, until she came upon a flight of familiar stairs. Up the stairs she capered, to find herself on the sunny streets of Paris.

Small crowds gathered on corners and under trees. A saxophone blew golden notes. A dancer stamped to the bouncy rhythm of banana drums and bongos.

Harmonica players, mimes, and bamboo flutists filled the sidewalks.

Near each performer lay an upside-down hat. Into the hats, smiling people dropped silver coins.

All day Sophie watched and listened, until the performers counted their coins and went home.

As evening approached, high-pitched music led Sophie to a sidewalk near the river and a man playing a fiddle. He shuffled his feet from time to time, but his legs were crooked and he could not lift them high.

His music was fast like the pace of the Metro. It made Sophie's feet move, the way they moved at breakfast in the morning rush.

Sophie jigged to a high note, jagged to a crescendo, then did a quick sidestep to the rollicking finish. Two people clapped their hands, tossed two silver coins into the man's empty hat, and walked on.

"You do a sprightly dance," said the fiddler to Sophie. "Once crowds came to watch my magic feet, but not anymore. Still, I can make a fiddle sing." Then, tipping his hat to Sophie, he said, "My name is Jacques. Tomorrow, if you like, join me. We will see if we make a good pair."

Dedicated to the fancy cat I met in the Paris Metro
and my two moms,
Elsie Raymond and Helen Arnold
—M. D. A.

For Cathy, Ray, and Michael Ann
—J. E. D.

Text copyright 2001 by Marsha Diane Arnold.
Illustrations copyright 2001 by Jack E. Davis.
All rights reserved. Printed in Italy.
No part of this book may be reproduced or copied in any form
without written permission from the publisher.
GOLDEN BOOKS®, A GOLDEN BOOK®,
GOLDEN BOOKS FAMILY STORYTIME™, and G DESIGN®
are trademarks of Golden Books Publishing Company, Inc.
A MMI

Library of Congress Cataloging-in-Publication Data
Arnold, Marsha Diane.
Metro cat / by Marsha Diane Arnold ; illustrated by Jack E. Davis.
p. cm.
Summary: When Sophie, the cover cat for Fancy Cat Magazine,
is stranded in a Paris Metro station, she must learn to fend for herself.
ISBN 0-307-10213-0 (alk. paper)
[1. Cats—Fiction. 2. Subways—France—Paris—Fiction. 3. Self-reliance—Fiction.
4. Paris (France)—Fiction.] I. Davis, Jack E., ill. II. Title.
PZ7.A7363 Me 2001   [E]—dc21   00-056173

*The illustrations for this book
were created with watercolor, acrylic, and colored pencil.*

Metro Cat

To Benjamin—
Fancy that!
Fancy Cat!

Marsha
Diane
Arnold

Meow
↑
Victoria

by MARSHA DIANE ARNOLD
illustrated by JACK E. DAVIS

A Golden Book ✧ New York

Golden Books Publishing Company, Inc., New York, New York 10106

Sophie LeBeque was the fanciest cat in Paris. Posters of her draped in diamond collars hung in Paris bus stops and store windows . . . even on the walls of the Metro, the Parisian subway.

Sophie led a hectic life as the Cover Cat for *Fancy Cat* magazine. She liked the attention. But the thing Sophie loved most about her life was her sunroom, where she ate fresh trout for breakfast, played in a catnip garden, and napped overlooking the River Seine.

One morning, Sophie's butler announced, "You
have a 7 A.M. photo session, Mademoiselle LeBeque!
We must hurry to catch the morning light at the Eiffel
Tower. I'll drape you in diamonds when we get there."

"I haven't had my fresh trout breakfast," meowed
Sophie.

But the butler did not hear. He placed Sophie in her

silk-lined carrying case, hurried to the limousine, and
sped into the streets of Paris. Sophie's cage slid from
side to side. "Please don't rush," she meowed.

But the limousine screeched around a corner, the
back door flew open, and Sophie's cage sailed out.

It bounced onto the street, teetered at the top of a
staircase, tumbled down . . .

BONG . . . BONG . . . BONG, jarred
open, and toppled Sophie into a swirling sea of shoes.
Sophie LeBeque, the fanciest cat in Paris, was in
the middle of the Metro's morning rush hour.

Pointy blue heels scrunched her toes.
Scruffy tennis shoes smashed her tail.
"MEOWCH!!!" shrieked Sophie.

A wave of brown loafers pushed Sophie further
down a long hallway. A swinging briefcase sent her
spinning into a corner.

Catching her breath, Sophie peered through the crowd. On the opposite wall was a poster of the June issue of *Fancy Cat* magazine, with Sophie posed next to the *Mona Lisa* at the Louvre.

Sophie meowed to the crowd, "I'm Sophie LeBeque, the fanciest cat in Paris. Please stop rushing and help me find my butler."

Click-click, squish-squish, shuffle-shuffle. The shoes rushed past.

Just then, Sophie's nose caught a tantalizing smell mingled with the scent of rubber soles and leather shoes. Running to catch their trains, the crowds munched breakfast. Here and there, a bit of baguette, a chunk of croissant, a piece of apple tart dropped between their shoes.

I didn't have my fresh trout this morning, Sophie remembered.

Cautiously, Sophie moved into the crowd.

She skipped by a sandal, leaped over a boot, and sidestepped an oxford to reach a taste of cream puff.

She scampered across a sneaker for a bite of chocolate crepe, darted around a platform shoe for a nibble of eclair, then scurried back to her corner and fell asleep, exhausted, on the floor.

The next day, Sophie tried to decide what to do. But her butler and *Fancy Cat* magazine had always told her what to do before. So in the Metro Sophie stayed.

She didn't like sleeping on the cold floor, and it was hectic rushing through shoes for breakfast. But Sophie made a game of when to rush in and when not to.

Soon she became so light on her feet that her paws were never scrunched and her tail never smashed. Twirling around a tennis shoe, swirling past a pump, and waltzing over a wingtip for a morsel of quiche became almost as much fun as playing in her catnip garden.

One morning after breakfast, Sophie noticed a man plastering a new poster on the wall, right over hers!

The morning light shone through the Eiffel Tower, making Monique's fur sparkle like her diamond collars.

Sophie LeBeque stared at the poster a long time.

But soon a familiar *click-click, squish-squish, shuffle-shuffle* sound entered her ears. She noticed a bit of baguette falling to the floor and rushed in after it.

Sophie scurried through one pair of shoes after another, until she came upon a flight of familiar stairs. Up the stairs she capered, to find herself on the sunny streets of Paris.

Small crowds gathered on corners and under trees. A saxophone blew golden notes. A dancer stamped to the bouncy rhythm of banana drums and bongos.

Harmonica players, mimes, and bamboo flutists filled the sidewalks.

Near each performer lay an upside-down hat. Into the hats, smiling people dropped silver coins.

All day Sophie watched and listened, until the performers counted their coins and went home.

As evening approached, high-pitched music led Sophie to a sidewalk near the river and a man playing a fiddle. He shuffled his feet from time to time, but his legs were crooked and he could not lift them high.

His music was fast like the pace of the Metro. It made Sophie's feet move, the way they moved at breakfast in the morning rush.

Sophie jigged to a high note, jagged to a crescendo, then did a quick sidestep to the rollicking finish. Two people clapped their hands, tossed two silver coins into the man's empty hat, and walked on.

"You do a sprightly dance," said the fiddler to Sophie. "Once crowds came to watch my magic feet, but not anymore. Still, I can make a fiddle sing." Then, tipping his hat to Sophie, he said, "My name is Jacques. Tomorrow, if you like, join me. We will see if we make a good pair."

Sophie watched Jacques amble down stone steps to the river and a faded houseboat. The deck shone in the moonlight. Fish splashed in the water. Somewhere in the air, Sophie thought she smelled the fragrance of catnip.

Sophie curled up on a bench to wait till morning.
She dreamed of the rushing people in the Metro,
people with lots of silver coins, but no music to hear.
She dreamed of dancing, but not by the river.

"Are you ready to see if we make a good pair?" Jacques called to Sophie in the morning.

Sophie padded and pawed in front of Jacques, moving in the direction of the Metro.

"You know another place to play music?" said Jacques. "Why not? Things could not get much worse than two coins in one day."

When they came to the Metro's entrance, Jacques scratched his head. "Music in the Metro?" But he followed Sophie down the stairs.

Sophie found a spot near her old corner and started her sidesteps. Jacques drew the bow slowly across his fiddle, then swayed it faster to an upbeat.

Click-click, squish-squish, shuffle-shuffle. The shoes rushed past.

Just as Sophie's paws began to burn and Jacques' arms began to ache, a small pair of shoes stopped in front of them. "Look, Mama, a dancing cat."

Sophie danced faster. Jacques played sweeter.

Click-click. Pointy heels paused. A thin woman with short black hair applauded, then dropped a coin in Jacques' hat.

Squish-squish. Scruffy tennis shoes stopped. A student munching French bread smiled and reached into his pocket for a coin. *Shuffle-shuffle.* A man in a brown overcoat tossed two coins.

Soon a sea of shoes surrounded Jacques and Sophie. By the end of the day, Jacques' hat was full. "We are a good pair," he said, winking at Sophie.

Today if you go to the Paris Metro, you will find it filled with tambourines and strumming guitars. But the favorites of the crowds are still Jacques the fiddler and Sophie LeBeque, the cat who brought music to the Metro.

Sophie likes being the Dancing Cat of the Metro.

But what she loves most is the warm deck of a faded houseboat, where she catches fresh trout for breakfast, dances in a catnip garden, and naps in the sun with Jacques, overlooking the River Seine.